Just because you are alone, doesn't mean you have to feel lonely!

MBoston

WHAT ABOUT ME?

WHAT ABOUT ME?

WRITTEN BY
MARC BOSTON

PICTURES BY
ANNIE WILKINSON

JUJU SEEDS

planting ideas of empowerment
www.jujuseeds.com
BALTIMORE ■ MARYLAND

ACKNOWLEDGEMENTS TO THE FOLLOWING INDIVIDUALS FOR THEIR CONTRIBUTION TO THIS BOOK:

EDITORS: BETSY BALLENGER AND C. JUMOKE BOSTON
ILLUSTRATOR: ANNIE WILKINSON
BOOK LAYOUT: MITCHELL&SENNAAR COMMUNICATIONS, INC.

VERY SPECIAL THANKS TO
RACHAEL BOSTON, C. JUMOKE BOSTON, JANE JACKSON, AND AMY LEE-TAI
FOR THEIR INVALUABLE CONTRIBUTIONS.

WHAT ABOUT ME?

ISBN-10: 0-9742052-3-0
ISBN-13: 978-0-9742052-3-6

PUBLISHED BY

JUJU SEEDS MEDIA, LLC.

P.O. BOX 2612

BALTIMORE, MD. 21215

I CAN HEAR THEM GIGGLING
IN THE OTHER ROOM.

THEY FORGOT ABOUT ME AGAIN,
I PRESUME.

I WALK UP TO THEM AND POLITELY SAY,
"WOULD IT BE OKAY WITH YOU IF I PLAY?"

BUT THEY DON'T HEAR ME SO I WALK AWAY.
GUESS THERE'S NO REASON FOR ME TO STAY.

I SUPPOSE I'M TOO SMALL
FOR THEM TO SEE.

IT'S TOUGH TO BE THE YOUNGEST OF THREE.

ANOTHER TEA PARTY AND I'M THE ONLY ATTENDEE.

THEY'RE HAVING FUN, BUT WHAT ABOUT ME?

THE FRONT DOOR SLAMS SHUT; THEY'VE DONE IT AGAIN.
THEY'RE OUTSIDE WITHOUT ME. IT SEEMS I CAN'T WIN!

I MUST HURRY TO CATCH THEM, BUT I CAN'T FIND MY SHOES.
WHY AM I THE LAST TO GET THE NEWS?

I LOOK OUT THE WINDOW AND WHAT DO I SEE?
BOTH OF MY SISTERS ARE CLIMBING A TREE.
AND I AM MISSING ANOTHER ACTIVITY.

THEY'RE HAVING FUN, BUT WHAT ABOUT ME?

I JUST WANT TO BE
A PART OF THE GROUP, YET IT
SEEMS LIKE I'M ALWAYS OUT OF THE LOOP.

I GUESS THEY DON'T CARE ABOUT HOW I FEEL,
BECAUSE THEY TREAT ME LIKE I'M A THIRD WHEEL.

AND I'M FINDING IT VERY HARD TO CONCEAL,
THAT THEIR BEHAVIOR TOWARDS ME IS LESS
THAN IDEAL.

I'M TRYING TO STAY CALM WITH GREAT DIFFICULTY
SINCE THEY'RE HAVING FUN, BUT WHAT ABOUT ME?

I DEMAND THAT THEY STOP LEAVING ME OUT,
AND IF THEY DON'T,
THEN I'M GOING TO SHOUT!

BUT THEY LOOK AT ME WITH CONFUSION AND DOUBT,
AS IF THEY DON'T KNOW
WHAT I'M TALKING ABOUT!

I'M GETTING QUITE PERTURBED YOU SEE,
THAT THEY ARE HAVING FUN,
BUT WHAT ABOUT ME?

MY SISTERS ACT LIKE
THEY'RE SUCH A BIG DEAL,
AS IF THEIR IDEAS HAVE
GREATER APPEAL.

BUT IT'S OK I'M ALONE,
I WON'T SIT HERE AND MOAN,
I'LL JUST MAKE UP A GAME ALL ON MY OWN.

I'LL PRETEND I'M A PIRATE, DOCTOR, OR AN ASTRONAUT;
OR WRITE A STORY WITH AN INTERESTING PLOT.

I CAN MAKE A DRESS OUT OF MOMMY'S BLUE BLOUSE,
OR TURN THE CHAIR CUSHIONS INTO A BOUNCY HOUSE!

WOW, I SEE I HAVE THE ABILITY
TO HAVE LOTS OF FUN,
EVEN THOUGH IT'S JUST ME.

SHHH, LISTEN, WHAT'S THAT SOUND?
IT'S MY BIG SISTERS WHO'VE COME
SNIFFING AROUND TO FIND OUT
WHAT HAS ME SO ENGROSSED.

"SEE I'M HAVING FUN TOO!" I PROUDLY BOAST.

"WE NEVER KNEW YOU WERE SO INVENTIVE,
WE'RE SORRY WE WERE INATTENTIVE.
SO LITTLE SISTER, WHAT DO YOU SAY?
DO YOU MIND IF WE COME AND PLAY?"

NOW THEY ARE FINALLY BEGINNING TO SEE,
THAT THEY WERE HAVING FUN
AND FORGOT ABOUT ME.

"YOU CERTAINLY CAN, LET'S MAKE IT A PLAN."

BUT THERE'S SOMETHING I'LL NEVER FORGET.
THAT BEING ALONE AND ALL BY MYSELF IS SURELY NOTHING TO FRET.

FOR THERE'S NO DEBATE, I HAVE THE POWER TO CREATE
ON MY OWN DEFINITELY!

AND I WON'T ELECT TO FEEL ANY NEGLECT OR EVER ASK, WHAT ABOUT ME.

FOR MARLEY, DELANEY, AND JOURNEY.

THANK YOU RACHAEL AND MOM
FOR ALL YOUR SUPPORT.

MARC BOSTON HAS ALWAYS BEEN A LOVER OF BOOKS
BUT DIDN'T GROW UP ASPIRING TO BECOME AN AUTHOR. HOWEVER
HE WAS INSPIRED TO WRITE ORIGINAL STORIES TO READ TO HIS
DAUGHTERS. WHAT ABOUT ME? IS HIS SECOND PUBLISHED CHILDREN'S
BOOK. MARC WAS BORN IN BALTIMORE, MD AND RAISED IN KANSAS
CITY, KS. HE LIVES WITH HIS WIFE RACHAEL AND THEIR THREE
DAUGHTERS IN CHARLOTTESVILLE, VA.

LOOK FOR MARC'S OTHER PUBLISHED BOOK,

THE GIRL WHO CARRIED TOO MUCH STUFF.